JUST BEFORE MIDNIGHT

A CHRISTMAS EVE NOVELLA

M.K. GILROY

JUST BEFORE MIDNIGHT

A CHRISTMAS EVE NOVELLA

SYDNEY
LANE
PRESS

Nashville, Tennessee

ISBN: 978-0-9721682-8-1 (eBook)
ISBN: 978-0-9721682-9-8 (Paperback)

Published by Sydney Lane Press,
a division of Gray Point Media LLC
2000 Mallory Lane, Suite 130-229
Franklin, Tennessee 37067
sydneylanepress.com

The characters in this novel are purely fictional and do not reflect the life and events of real individuals.

Version 2.14.11.10

Printed in the United States of America

Dedicated to Merrick & Naomi Gilroy.

Thanks Mom and Dad!

M.K. Gilroy Novels

The Kristen Conner Mystery Series:
Cuts Like a Knife
Every Breath You Take
Cold As Ice

Prologue

Roger was driving too fast. The back end of his long sleek automobile started to slide out to his left. His stomach balled in a knot at the thought he might spin in circles until the car jumped the curb and hit a street lamp, telephone pole or worse.

He cut the wheel left to correct the slide, taking him across the centerline as two headlights raced toward him, barreling down the treacherous city street straight at him even faster than he was driving. The front bumper of the approaching missile was dragging on the asphalt like a snowplow, shooting sparks despite the wet and icy conditions.

Dear Lord.

His life didn't pass before his eyes but he felt a tremor of fear, certain a high-speed head-on collision was inevitable and that he was going to die along with everyone else in the car in a fiery ball of flame.

His front wheels caught traction with a shudder and he jerked the wheel right, then left, easing out of the slide and back into his own lane of traffic.

His heart was banging a hard staccato rhythm. It felt like a bass drum.

He heard her crying softly, whimpering in the back seat, interrupted by a series of quick pants, then followed by a long, loud moan of pain.

He started to turn to her out of instinct, but reminded himself, just keep your eyes on the road. All you can do for her now is drive.

His hands gripped the leather wheel of the BMW M6 Gran Coupe. For once he didn't feel guilty about all the money he spent on the automobile he bought as a retirement gift to himself. An extravagance his wife had said. His sons and daughter thought it was great and about time he splurged on himself.

Roger had pictured himself in the silver streak powering through tight turns on a winding road in the mountains—dry pavement all the way—not as part of a life-or-death dash through slushy, icy urban streets.

It hadn't snowed for a couple days, but a light precipitation started earlier in what had seemed to be a glorious—and blessedly calm—Christmas Eve. Then the temperature dropped twenty degrees below the freezing point as night fell. The roads seemed fairly clear when he and his wife Margaret first started driving earlier in the evening, but now patches of hidden ice reached up and robbed the performance sedan of its footing.

He glanced to his right. His wife of forty years was on her knees on the seat facing backwards. The last time she hadn't worn a seatbelt was probably when they were dating. She was careful and cautious. Those weren't options in current circumstances.

Margaret was leaning as far as she could through the gap into the back seat, holding hands with and cooing words of reassurance to ... well, he didn't know the young woman's name. He wasn't sure how old she was either. He couldn't tell anymore. Maybe eighteen. Maybe twenty-five.

Have I seen her before? She does look familiar.

The man next to her was hurt as well. He had a gash on his left temple that was still seeping blood. He held Roger's white handkerchief to his wound. His eyes were clinched tight. His lips moved in a steady rhythm. Was he praying?

We all need to be praying.

Roger didn't drink coffee in his Beamer for fear of spills. A man bleeding all over his white leather upholstery and light charcoal carpet would have made the rule laughable; except a real flesh and blood man was bleeding.

Eyes on the road. Just drive.

He slowed as he approached the intersection and then gunned through it despite the red light. Under the circumstances he was certain he wouldn't get a traffic citation. The police and all emergency services, including ambulances, were tied up in an inferno down in the warehouse district.

Traffic was light. It was almost midnight and bitterly cold. Most people would be snug at home, finishing last minute wrapping of presents to be ripped open on Christmas morning. Maybe watching "It's a Wonderful Life" or "Home Alone" or "White Christmas" or another holiday favorite. Some families might be out at a Christmas Eve service at church, but downtown was closed off and it appeared midtown was already half asleep.

Except for those crazy kids driving a wrecked car.

A thought flickered in his mind … was that the car that hit … but he stopped thinking. He needed to keep his focus on the task at hand.

He sped toward another intersection, the light turning yellow one hundred feet before he arrived. His right foot went toward the brake but he didn't see headlight beams coming from either side, so he accelerated hard. His stomach knotted again.

What in the heck am I doing? How did I get in the middle of this?

He barely eased off the accelerator as his body was tugged hard right while he rounded the corner hard. Then he tensed and gasped as the rear end fishtailed again. He heard his wife bump the side door with her head and another gasp of pain from both of the backseat passengers.

He turned the wheel deftly into the slide and the car straightened out. Despite the blood and tears and whimpers and sobs from the backseat he lifted his foot off the accelerator. He had no choice. He was beginning to feel lightheaded from the stress.

I am going to get her there safe and sound—and then I'll go sit down, relax, and enjoy a hard earned heart attack. You always wanted a big, fast, power car. Apparently you needed it more than you knew.

Just drive.

Should be there in less than three minutes. Maybe four. This is going to turn out okay.

Then she let out a wail that pierced his body to the bone. He felt a sparkle of electricity race up his spine. The hairs on his neck stood on end.

"Hit it Rog, the baby is coming," Margaret said calmly next to him. It was the only time he could remember her ever telling him to drive faster.

He stomped his foot hard on the accelerator as the needle darted from forty-five to eighty-five in a thirty-five-mile-per-hour zone.

He had always wanted to do that but had been too afraid to try. Now he knew why. Signs and telephone posts and store fronts flashed by in a blur of colors and shadows.

The lights of St. Elizabeth were ahead, shimmering in the misty night air like a mirage. They always put a star on the bell tower during Christmas season. Now it was his beacon. He was no wise man, he thought to himself, but he knew enough to drive as fast as he could toward the star.

The young woman's scream became a nonstop clanging and echoing in his head.

So close. So far away. But this is going to turn out okay. Whatever your name is, please be okay. I'm doing the best I can.

"Stay with us honey, stay with us!" Margaret called, her voice rising and breaking.

Dear Lord, I need some help right now. Please. Right now.

1

Fourteen Hours Earlier

I'm sorry, sir," but your card has been declined.

She tried to look cheerful and casual. But her smile was so forced it looked like a cartoon grimace. She was a nice lady. She obviously felt bad and was embarrassed for him. She would make this financial transaction work for him if she could. He could feel her goodness like an aura surrounding her. But somehow that didn't help him feel better. It made his situation feel even worse.

His shift was about to start and he didn't have more than a few bucks of cash on him, just enough to get a cup of coffee before he got in line at the airport to pick up early afternoon passengers, arriving home for the holidays.

He was sure he had at least $50 on his debit card, the only rectangle of plastic he had left in his wallet. But he hadn't checked his account on the computer in the common room outside the dispatcher's office. He meant to. Another mistake in a mistake-filled life.

He had figured it would be a great tip day and he could pay expenses the next few days with cash. He wouldn't have a direct deposit from Acme Cab in his checking account until the 31st.

I was being careful with money all month. Where did it go?

His mind whirled as blood rushed to his face, the body's confession of his failure and humiliation.

I pick up the kids at seven. It's my year to have Christmas with them. When am I going to have time to find something for them before then?

His purchase had come to forty bucks. Two gifts for each of them. It wasn't much but it was all he could do. Apparently it was more than he could do.

"Let me get that," the lady behind him in line whispered, thrusting her credit card toward the cashier.

Every ounce of pride he had left in his spirit wanted to say no. Scream no. But he lowered his head and mumbled, "thanks."

He thought of the beggars working intersections with cardboard signs telling drivers that they were a homeless vet or Jesus loved them or they would work for food or they planned to buy booze. Is that how far he had fallen?

His eyes were moist as he gathered the two plastic bags from the small carousel next to the checkout station.

"Thank you," he said, trying to make eye contact with

the lady who bought his children's toys, but not quite succeeding when he saw the concern and sympathy in the eyes of his benefactor. Sometimes kindness hurt as much as cruelty. It reminded you how needy you were.

He headed for the exit in a daze; too numb to succumb to the tears he felt welling.

How had his life come to this? What was next? What else could go wrong?

It's Christmas Eve and you've got your kids starting tonight. That's all that matters. It's going to be good. Again.

2

Thirteen Hours Earlier

Is this still a dream or is someone pounding on my front door?

Regina woke with a start. She groaned at the interruption to her sleep. She sighed. She was going to have to get up in an hour to get ready for work anyway.

It didn't seem right with her seniority that she had to pull a twelve-hour shift in the emergency room from 2:00 p.m. on Christmas Eve to 2:00 a.m. on Christmas morning. Who knows, she thought. This is the season of peace on earth and good will to men, so it might be quiet. But things don't always turn out the way we hoped.

Including now. Someone was banging on her front door.

She pulled on a robe and grumbled all the way to the front door. Where was Douglas when she needed him?

She looked through the spy hole and her heart sank. The police. And Donny.

Sixteen-year-old Donny. Her baby. Two older brothers already out of the house, one in Afghanistan and one in his senior year of college. Neither gave her and Douglas more than a little trouble, the kind of trouble you expected from rambunctious boys. The kind of trouble that sometimes made you laugh, even if you weren't going to let your boys see you smile.

But not Donny. School suspensions, police warnings, and one arrest. The arrest was filed in Juvenile Court. It was to be destroyed if he kept his nose clean for the next two years. He had eighteen months to go. Even through a tiny circular spyhole drilled into her front door she didn't think Donny's nose looked very clean.

She smoothed her mess of hair back and pulled the door open.

"Yes?"

"Good morning, are you Mrs. Bennett, Ma'am?"

Regina realized what she must look like to the two men in blue that knocked on doors where there was almost always a problem waiting to greet them. Her hair was a mess. The living room was cluttered with pizza boxes and pop cans—Douglas had ordered a midnight snack for Donny and his friends while she was at work. No one thought to clean up after themselves. And here she was in her rattiest pajamas and a frayed bathrobe just before 11:00 a.m. She knew the officer was doing his best to be polite, but she felt the vibe. He was thinking she was a derelict mother who didn't know what was going on with her wayward son. With the way she was sure she looked, he might be thinking she was sleeping off a holiday hangover.

"I'm Regina Bennett, Officer. Is there a problem?"

She looked past him and couldn't help but glare at Donny. Donny kept his eyes fixed on the top of his tennis shoes and refused to make eye contact.

Where is Douglas? Where is he when I need him? He hasn't worked in six months. He's at JavaStar on his laptop pretending he is applying for jobs. He's probably doing the Crossword. Or Sudoku. I'm paying the bills, cleaning up messes, and dealing with a son that doesn't want to be dealt with.

"There is, Mrs. Bennett. May we come in?"

She nodded her head numbly and led the two officers and Donny into the kitchen. Thank the Good Lord it was clean and picked up, she thought. That's because Douglas and Donny hadn't gone near it.

"Cup of coffee?" she asked.

"If it's not too much trouble," the officer responded.

Uh oh. He plans to be here for a while.

"I work over at St. Elizabeth's and was about to put the pot on anyway," she said, moving over to a cupboard to scoop the dark ground beans into a copper filter. The water was already in the chamber of her Mr. Coffeemaker.

"Excuse me for not introducing myself, Mrs. Bennett,

I'm Officer Jamie Carver and this is my partner, Todd King."

"So what's happened?" Regina asked.

"Your son and several of his friends ate breakfast this morning and left the restaurant without paying. They stopped at a gas station and filled the tank of an SUV and drove off, again, without paying."

"Hugh and Scott and Duane?" she asked Donny.

He looked like he might mumble something but kept his eyes glued on the wood swirls of the tabletop.

"You know I told you you had to stop hanging with them."

Donny didn't answer.

"You sure Donny was with them?" she asked Carver.

"Yes. He had a nice big smile for the security cameras in both places."

Regina sighed. Not only did her son get in trouble, he almost always got caught. Or maybe he got in even more trouble than she suspected.

The door from the small one-car garage banged open as Douglas called in a singsong voice, "Merry Christmas. Santa's home! If you've been good, he just might have a nice present for you!"

His face changed from jolly to somber in the split second he saw the police officers with Donny and Regina at the table.

"What's going on?"

"You gonna tell your dad, Donny?"

"We can help you if you cooperate, Donny," the second officer said.

So Donny deadpanned what happened to his dad, never making eye contact. How many times have we told him it's time to man up and look people in the eye? The second officer, Regina had already forgotten his name, took notes.

"Do we need a lawyer?" Douglas asked. "What happens next?"

"We want to work with you," Officer Carver said. "What happens next depends on whether we can work out a plan with Donny that includes some apologies and restitution payments. Then we want him under parent supervision. Will one of you be here all evening?"

Regina and Douglas nodded.

"I'm working the ER at St. E's tonight, but those two will," Regina said, looking pointedly at father and son. "They aren't going anywhere."

3

Twelve Hours Earlier

Margaret, don't look so sad. I've never seen you mope around so much."

"I'm trying, Roger. I just miss the kids so much."

"It's Christmas Eve. We knew this day was coming. Our kids are married. Now we have to share them. The in-laws want them home for Christmas too. We'll call them in the morning and you can talk to everybody for hours."

"I don't want to talk to them on the phone. I want them here," she said softly. "And I want my grandbabies."

Roger sighed. He was doing his best to stay positive, but he was feeling the same sense of absence and loneliness Margaret was.

"We knew this day was coming when Trish got married this summer. It made sense for her and Barry to be on the same Christmas rotation as the others. We have all the kids and grandkids next year."

"Roger, I'm so glad you love me enough to try and cheer me up. But you keep telling me things I already know. I know the kids are where they are supposed to be. I'm just feeling a little ... selfish. No, I'm feeling a *lot* selfish. I want my grandbabies here in the flesh. Yesterday."

A thought crossed Roger's mind.

"So this is all about you feeling selfish?"

"Roger, I'm not in the mood to joke."

"How selfish?"

"Roger, it's Christmas Eve and I'm about to say something I'll regret later," she said with rolled eyes as she headed into the kitchen.

Determined, he followed.

"Since we can't have what we want most, let's be selfish this year," he pressed on.

"I have no clue what you are talking about."

"Give me a fifteen minutes and I'll be back and explain," he said, a twinkle in his eye.

Margaret pulled a pan of cornbread she had made to go with a small pot of chili on the stove as Roger reentered the kitchen thirty minutes later with a look of triumph.

What is he up to? He looks like the cat that swallowed the canary.

She tasted the chili. Just okay. Why was it so much harder to cook for two than to cook for a group? If the kids and their spouses and the grandkids were here it would have been the large soup pot on the stovetop with a lot of extra fixings and an array of side dishes and desserts to go with it she thought glumly.

Margaret had heard the computer printer grinding away and spitting out pages a few minutes earlier. Roger held two a small sheaves of papers to his chest. He cleared his throat but didn't say anything as she ladled chili into the first earthenware bowl. He obviously wanted her to ask what he had come up with but she made him wait. She wasn't feeling cooperative.

He cleared his throat again.

"Are you going to get around to asking?" he said in mock anger.

"What have you got Roger?" she asked, setting the bowl down and looking up.

"Something very selfish."

She turned off the oven and turned to her husband. "I told you I'm not in the mood for joking today."

"Neither am I."

"Okay, don't drag this out. What have you got?"

"Two tickets to London," he said with a smile. "How soon can you pack? We're taking the redeye tonight."

"You're not serious, Roger."

"But I am. See for yourself."

"You had to spend a fortune to get last minute tickets. In First Class."

"I've got so many unused miles that the tickets were

free, though there was a hefty little expedite fee. The hotel is a fortune, however."

"Tonight? You can't be serious. We don't have time."

"We have nothing else to do today. Right?"

"Right ... but this is so sudden."

"You've always said I'm impatient."

"True."

"Christmas in London is something you've always wanted to do. So let's do it. I'm sure someone is doing Dickens' 'Christmas Carol' on the West End. Where better to see it than London? We have no kids to worry about, so let's make the most of it. I can't think of a better year to go."

She put her hands on her hips, ready to scold her husband.

This is crazy. Just up and fly to London? I have wanted to see London over the Christmas holidays ...

She hugged him, planted a big kiss on his neck, and said, "You're going to have to serve your own lunch. I've got packing to do."

She took the bowl of chili and headed down the hall to the bedroom, her mind whirling.

"I couldn't get a room at The Savoy so we're staying at the Milestone across from Kensington Palace," Roger called to her back.

She really didn't care where they stayed. This really

was crazy. London. It would be a cold, wet, windy mess at Christmas. But the lights would be marvelous. She loved taking the Tube but they might have to take cabs wherever they wanted to sightsee to stay out of the weather. She wondered if Harrods had half off sales like stores in the States did after Christmas. She would have to find out. She really had wanted to go to London for Christmas one year.

Roger was right. This really was the best time to do it. And the airfare was free.

"Margaret!" she heard him call from down the hall. "I'm going to run to the mall and pick up a few things for the trip. Do you want me to pick up that hot peppermint drink you like at JavaStar?"

She popped her head out the bedroom door and said, "No thanks. It'll get cold before you're home. You better get in and out of the mall areas as fast as you can. People turn into maniacs when they are stuck with last minute shopping—and you are one of them."

She'd never heard of the Milestone. She wondered how much it was per night. Then she decided she didn't want to know.

When do I tell Roger and the kids the news I got yesterday? I don't want to mess up the holidays for anyone else.

4

Eleven Hours Earlier

She couldn't keep doing this. This had to be her last day to work. But even when she thought she had cut all the fat out of her meager budget, the money Brad sent home and her small paycheck every two weeks didn't go far enough.

If only he could be home now. At Christmas last year he had been certain he would be home for good six months ago—4th of July at the latest—but there were still seventy thousand U.S. soldiers in Afghanistan. Right in the middle of it all was Brad's company, the Army First—the Big Red One Brad loved to call it. He knew she didn't like it when he called it by its other nickname: The Bloody First.

Her job at the JavaStar outside the mall was fine. Holly had worked her way from the cash register to barista the past year. But being on her feet all day was murder. The baby was due in two weeks. A lot of women work all the way up to the delivery her OB-GYN told her cheerfully.

Most had jobs where they could sit down most of

the day she wanted to answer.

She rubbed her belly and looked down to try and find her feet.

Probably better I can't see them anymore. My ankles are hideous. Well that might not be entirely true. I'm not sure I have ankles anymore.

They will ache tonight.

All she wanted was to be home, her feet propped up, and Brad back home and safe. Beside her. She wanted his arms around her. She didn't care if he was watching football or reading a book. She just wanted his presence with her and the baby.

He went to his CO to appeal for an extended leave before Christmas but was turned down since he would be coming home closer to the birth of the baby anyway. They couldn't spare him for two weeks?

And what if the baby comes early? He probably won't, but what if he does? That would be only one extra week.

She hated the thought of being alone for Christmas. Her mom was going to try and drive up, but said she didn't have enough vacation time to make the trip and then come back when the baby was born.

I'm glad you are coming for the baby Mom, but what about me?

Things hadn't been the same between Holly and

her mom since she married Brad just after she finished JuCo. The plan was to wait until she finished her BA from a four-year-college. She gave it the old college try for a semester, but with Brad months from deployment, the two couldn't wait any longer.

They thought getting married would make finishing college for her easier. He had few expenses on his tour of duty and was able to send most of what he made back home. But then the little strip of paper turned blue and life got a little more complicated.

Despite her mom's disapproval Holly didn't regret her decision for a moment. Even if her mom was right. Yes, it was a rash decision. Maybe a little foolish. But weren't you supposed to be a little foolish when you fell in love?

Brad had a history degree from A&M and planned on being a teacher when he opted out of the Army. He wanted to coach. But as a member of the ROTC his way through college was paid by Uncle Sam. Even though he had no student loans to contend with, there was still a bill to be paid. It came due immediately after he walked off the stage at graduation. With a major of shortage of officers, there was no question where his first assignment would be as a newly commissioned lieutenant first class.

She let him know she was pregnant a week before

he left. Then she called to let her mom know. Her tears and words—"you are screwing up your life"—still ached inside her, right next to the baby.

Holly's mom raised her as a single parent and she and Holly had always been close. Her mom had hammered a college degree in her head. Marriage and pregnancy had put a strain between them they had never experienced and that Holly could hardly believe.

Her mom raised her to know right and wrong. Taught her to be kind, forgiving, and generous. She had modeled those ideals too. But her disappointment in Holly going a different route than planned—actually the route she herself had taken and that hadn't worked out—had drive an icy wedge that left Holly feeling so alone.

Something's gotta give. She's going to accept all this and be herself again so we can be close again.

Her mom swore that it wasn't the reason, but Holly couldn't help but believe that disappointment in her was why Mom had taken a job transfer two states away. She couldn't bear to see all she had worked and planned and hoped for with Holly change so dramatically.

Don't I get to have a say in my life and my future, Mom?

She looked down at the thermostat popping out of the silver frother she steamed the milk in. 160 degrees.

Ready to pour over two shots of espresso. She had gotten quite good at making a leaf design from the foamy milk on the surface.

She looked up and a man was glaring at her.

"Did you make my drink?"

"I don't know. Probably so," she said hesitantly.

Gerald was making drinks, too, but he had disappeared in the back room for a second.

"Well you screwed it up royally," he nearly shouted. "I asked for an extra shot of espresso and I asked for it extra hot. What I got is weak and lukewarm."

Holly bit her lip. "Let me make that for you again, sir."

"I'm working, so I want it done next," he demanded.

"Yes, sir."

"I don't have time for this. I wouldn't think making a strong, hot cup of coffee was rocket science."

Holly felt like a hippopotamus waddling over to the window to hand the drink she had just finished to Gwynn, who was working the drive thru.

"If you don't spit in his drink, I will," Gwynn whispered, giving Holly a sad little wink and squeezing her hand.

Holly took a deep breath, fought back a tear, and turned back. People were shaking their heads and looking at her in sympathy.

"Don't let this get you down for Christmas, young lady," a kindly older gentleman with white hair said to her, concern in his eyes.

She looked around with the freshly made latte. The man that had yelled at her was gone.

5

Ten Hours Earlier

I hope we have something besides turkey tomorrow," she said to her husband.

"Why even bring it up?" he said back to her. "You know my mom is going to bake a turkey."

"Turkey is for Thanksgiving. Couldn't we have something else for Christmas?"

"Don't bring it up."

She sighed. "And I hope your sister's kids aren't going to be monsters again this year."

"They're kids. Kids are monsters."

They both laughed at that.

This is nauseating, Joe thought, glancing in the rearview mirror.

"And that's why we aren't going to have kids," she said.

Joe turned into a cul-de-sac and the man said, "Last house on the right. The one with the plastic reindeer and sleigh out front."

That got the couple laughing again.

"Your parents are a hoot, Daniel," she said, almost

crying from her laughter. "Where did you find them?"

Yeah, yeah, real funny.

"The stork brought them," he answered. "I've been looking at that same set of decorations since I was young enough to believe my dad when he told me Santa kept his sleigh parked in our front yard."

Joe's stomach did a somersault as he wondered if there would be any turkeys left at Kroger. Just the three of us he thought, doesn't have to be a big one.

He pulled into the driveway, popped the trunk lid, and lifted out two roller board suitcases as an elderly couple ambled forward with beaming smiles to hug their son and daughter-in-law.

"Do you take a credit card?" the son asked.

Joe's heart sank. With a credit card, his tip money would show up on his 31st paycheck. He needed it now.

Before he could tell him it was no problem, the dad said, "I got this. You paid for the airline tickets. I can get the cab. I still can't believe my doctor won't let me drive so I can come to the airport to get you myself."

"It's no problem Dad."

"Get your stuff inside."

"Dad, let me—" the son started to protest but then two kids raced from the side of the house yelling, "Uncle Danny!" at the top of their lungs and chucking snowballs. Daniel ducked, smiled, and scooped the kids up as his wife moved away quickly to avoid the flurry of wet arms and legs.

"How much?" the father asked Joe with a twinkle in his eyes.

"Fifty-five bucks," Joe answered.

Did the man stiffen? Fifty-five bucks sounded like a lot. People didn't understand what the price of gas and insurance had done to a simple cab fare.

The man pulled out four twenties, then fixed him with a smile, and said, "Merry Christmas."

Joe reached for his wallet to get change but the man squeezed his arm and said, "Let's call it even," before heading back to the front door.

"Merry Christmas to you too, sir."

The man didn't turn back. He probably didn't hear him. Might be hard of hearing or maybe Joe's voice had gone soft.

For the third time that day Joe felt tears welling in his eyes. Twice from humiliation. This time from gratitude.

I'm glad your daughter gave you kids and I hope your daughter-in-law knows how blessed you all are to have kids running around the house. They're not monsters. They're angels. And I will have my angels soon.

It was his fourth fare of the day and three of his customers had tipped in cash. He needed cash. Maybe it would be a merry Christmas after all.

He backed out of the drive, shifted into drive, and pulled forward.

His kids—his angels and the only thing he seemed to have to live for—liked to decorate cookies. He would make it a Christmas morning activity. They would bake the cookies in reindeer, star, tree, wreath, sleigh, and other holiday shapes. After the cookies cooled, the three of them would make a huge mess decorating them with different icing colors and sparkles and Red Hots and M&Ms and anything else they could think of.

He felt hopeful. The kids would love it. He used to be good at stuff like this.

He might have enough cash to take them to the movie theatre the next day.

He started adding up ticket prices and popcorn in his mind and thought he might be able to nab one more fare to be sure he had enough cash on hand. He would hustle home and get cleaned up before picking Jonathan and Leslie up.

I'll just rent a couple videos from the box outside McDonalds. I'll bet there will be nonstop holiday movies on regular TV we can watch. Might be better than going to the movie theatre and fighting the crowds.

Whatever makes them happy.

Joe just hoped Kroger had at least one small turkey left.

His stomach twisted and lurched as he replayed the scene of him yelling at the girl at JavaStar. She really had screwed up his coffee drink, which shouldn't have happened.

But how was I to know she was pregnant?

Just how far had he fallen? This was the bottom wasn't it?

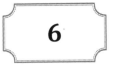

6

Nine Hours Earlier

Second degree burns on his right arm and shoulder. Poor little guy. Six-years-old, that age when little boys are going to climb, no matter how many times you tell them not to. Her boys had all climbed. Troy had a couple stitches on his chin from falling off the kitchen table when he was three. Jason broke her favorite lamp with a donkey kick from jumping off an end table onto the couch. Donny never got hurt. But if he went missing as a little kid, the first place to look was up; he was usually in the top branches of the maple tree in the front yard.

Apparently little Eduardo was excited that all his cousins were at his house and thought it would be a good idea to pull the pan drawer out from under the stove to use as a step, then chin himself up to see what smelled so good up there. He pulled a pot of apple cider off the stovetop. Thank God only a few splashes hit his face. But Eduardo would have some permanent scars down the shoulder and arm.

Eduardo would never forget this Christmas. It was going to be painful and he wasn't going to spend it at home with his cousins.

He was sleeping like an angel now, heavily sedated. Nothing was harder in her profession than hearing the scream of a child in pain.

Regina brushed a tear out of her eye. What had happened to her sweet little Donny? He was such a good little boy. When did he start getting in trouble? Twelve? Thirteen? Boys get in trouble, but with him, his attitude went south so hard and so fast. Maybe Troy and Jason spoiled her and Douglas. Even when they disobeyed they were charming ... and even respectful if that is possible. It didn't help that Douglas had been laid off for six months. Being out of work had been hard on him. On her. On their marriage. Whether Donny would have shown more respect to his dad if he was still first shift foreman on the assembly line at AppWorks, she didn't know.

Donny was sixteen and responsible for his own actions. She didn't want to blame others for his shortcomings, but once he hit his last year of middle school and had become constant friends with Hugh, Scott, and Duane—especially Duane—whatever problems were already there had gotten worse. Much worse. He might join his brother in Afghanistan, but for entirely different motives and on an entirely different path.

All Jason had ever wanted to be was an Army Ranger. When he wrestled and played lacrosse in high school, he loved the team camaraderie and was competitive as anyone. But his drive was always to be ready to blow through physical testing so he could be part of some type of special ops division.

Regina watched little Eduardo, sleeping. The doctor wanted the place quiet and had tried to send everyone home. But his momma wasn't leaving.

Regina's phone vibrated and when she saw Douglas's number she stepped out into the hall and picked up quickly.

"What's the story?"

"I think we got off a lot easier than we deserved. No charges."

"How did you pull that off?"

"Got all four boys over here. Officer Carver went with me, Hugh's dad, and the boys to the restaurant and the gas station. We made restitution and the boys apologized. Very nicely I might add."

"Where were Duane and Scott's folks?"

"Duane's mom is at work and you know there's no dad there. Scott's dad was at work, too."

"And there's no mom there."

"Bingo."

"Are they going to pay us back?"

"I'll work on that, but frankly that's the least of my worries right now."

"Money doesn't grow on trees you know, Douglas. Especially not these days."

"Okay Regina, I will let you know when we'll get paid back when I know. I do know where this conversation is going, so I'm signing off now."

"I've got more questions," Regina said to nobody. The line was dead.

Why in the world did I start a fight she wondered? No charges. I should be happy. Or at least not as miserable.

Still, he shouldn't have hung up.

The out-of-date PA system squawked and a tinny voice said, "EMTs are making a special delivery. Critical condition. Assumed heart attack. Staff to front bay."

Still not too busy in the St. Elizabeth ER. But there's still a little sun light outside. Give it some time.

It's Christmas Eve. Why did I start a fight with Douglas? He did good.

7

Eight Hours Earlier

Blame it on your dad. I can't believe it either."

"I miss you gwandma," a bubbly voice interrupted, with little Rachel's face taking over the computer screen.

How had they lived before the age of PCs and Skype and Facebook and one hundred other ways to stay connected? Roger would tell her that in the early days of video conferencing, it could cost his legal firm a thousand bucks an hour to connect face-to-face remotely. Now she and Roger had their own Skype account that did the same thing for free.

Seeing Rachel's face—despite a finger in her nose—gave Margaret a sharp pang of sadness that not even a dream trip to London could mask.

"Tell everyone I said goodbye and am off to pack," Roger called from behind her.

"You okay Mom?" her oldest child, Megan, asked.

Margaret wiped a tear and tried to smile, but then couldn't stem the flow of tears that broke the dam and flooded.

"Mom ..."

"I'm all right."

"You and daddy are going to have a blast. I'm jealous."

"I know. I know. It was so sweet of him to come up with something like this for me. Though I wish he hadn't spent so much money."

"Mom, you always worry about money. Dad made a fortune. You're loaded."

"I know. But I think part of the reason we're loaded is because I always worried about it."

They both laughed at that.

"Mom, we love you. Go finish packing. Scratch that. I know you're already packed. Go help daddy or nothing will match. Ever since he retired his navy blue Brooks Brothers suit with white shirt and red power tie, he's a mess. He'd be lost without you."

"It wasn't just the suits that made him look so distinguished Meg. I had to match his ties and socks too."

They both laughed again, but it was a fading laugh, and there wasn't much left to say.

"Mom, I miss you. Next Christmas will be wonderful. Now go make sure Dad doesn't pack his golf pants for the theatre in the dead of winter."

Margaret shuddered at the word dead. Who knows the future? Who knows if there will be a next Christmas with all those you love? Nothing in life is guaranteed.

The doctor said to enjoy the holidays. To not worry.

That this was very treatable.

But what if it wasn't? Would Roger be okay? Of course he would, even if he didn't match.

Stop being so morbid. It is almost Christmas. Be joyful. Christmas is a time of joy.

She would tell Roger and the kids after she and Roger got back from London.

"Hug the kids and Jeff for me."

"I will Mom."

She moved the cursor to the red "end call" button on the computer screen. She'd never been good at hanging up the telephone. Seeing Meg's face so close but so far away made it even harder.

The kids are happy where they are, which is as it should be. They're going to have a marvelous time. So are you and Roger. Feel happy. Nothing can spoil the holidays.

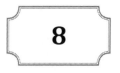

8

Seven Hours Earlier

The call went straight into voice mail. Her mom forgot to charge her phone sometimes. A lot. But surely she was going to call her wasn't she? It was Christmas Eve. Holly had never felt so alone in her life.

When her manager asked if she wanted to take the rest of the day off after the angry man yelled at her, she demurred. Then he insisted. Kindly but firmly. She thought she could put the tirade behind her, but tears came so easily these days. She didn't blame her manager for wanting her out of the store. People came to JavaStar to pay extra for a coffee drink so they could savor the warmth of the season. Seeing the barista with red swollen eyes wasn't warm and cheerful.

She looked at her ankles propped up on the couch. Thank God customers couldn't see them.

It didn't help that she made a quick stop inside the mall to pick up a candle. Her tiny studio apartment was decorated but she needed something, anything to try and drive out the gloom she felt.

It was there she saw two girls she had class with

when she was in her first year of junior college. Erica and Danielle. She was surprised they didn't hurt themselves when they saw it was her. Both of their jaws dropped wide open.

"Holly, look at you," Erica said.

Danielle tried harder to recover: "You look wonderful, Holly. They're right. A pregnant woman just glows."

Danielle really was trying. The words just wouldn't flow.

"When is it coming?" Erica asked.

It?

"He'll be here in about two weeks," Holly had answered.

"You gotta carry that thing for two more weeks?" Erica exclaimed, horror stricken before turning beet red when she realized how bad she sounded.

"That's what the doctor said. Two more weeks. But I think I've passed the point of glowing, Danni."

"You look like an angel," Danielle said. "You gotta call us when the baby is born so we can come visit."

"I'd heard you got married but I didn't hear you were pregnant," Erica added.

She looked at Erica's furrowed brow and wondered if she was she doing math in her head to see if she had to get married.

She hadn't.

"I wish we would have known so we could have come to the shower."

"I would have loved that," Holly said, not feeling her words.

She didn't tell them there was no shower. She lived almost an hour from where she grew up. The small church she attended all her life would have thrown a shower for her, complete with folding chairs, a white frosted cake, and a plastic punch bowl fashioned like it was cut from fine crystal. But it was too far away for her to attend and with her mom out-of-town now she was out of touch with the only people she seemed to know. She went to a great church but it was really big and she didn't know that many people.

Brad grew up in Texas in a broken home and wasn't close to either of his parents so no one was looking out for her from that direction.

Once she married Brad, she had basically lost track of most of her friends. So there was no one to even think about planning a shower.

She assumed that once Brad was home they would make lots of friends together. This was a temporary state of loneliness.

I hope.

"Holly, promise you'll call when the baby comes,"

Danielle said. "I mean it. We'll get some of the gang together."

"I'd love that," she repeated.

She watched the two skinny girls sashay off, laughing loud and whispering softly in each other's ears.

I'm not jealous. I don't think. But I do feel like a hippopotamus.

She had hurried home in eager anticipation of the email Brad sent every day before he started his day twelve hours ahead of her. But when she got home there was no email waiting for her. That worried here. He always assured her that he wasn't "outside the wire" and was probably in the safest spot in all of Afghanistan. His job was logistics, which meant moving supplies from Iraq to Afghanistan and rerouting them back to 82nd Airborne Division in Fort Bragg, North Carolina.

That doesn't mean I don't worry every minute of every day. It was still a war zone.

She rubbed her belly. The baby kicked and that made her smile.

He's telling me I'm not alone. He's going to be here in two weeks. And Brad.

Then he kicked again and it felt like he did a gymnastic twist and turn.

She tried to hold the smile but it hurt too much.

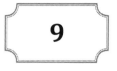

9

Six Hours Earlier

Y ou call this a tip?"

"Consider yourself lucky pal. I told you I was in a hurry and you drove slower than my grandma."

"Then your grandma must be a NASCAR driver."

"Funny guy. Not. No wonder you drive a cab."

"A thirty dollar fare and you give me your loose change?"

"More than you deserve. Consider it a tip on listening to the customer."

Joe's hands balled into fists.

If this clown knew what I used to do and be.

That was the problem. He had just turned forty and Joe's best days seemed to be a distant speck in the rearview mirror.

"Go ahead tough guy, throw a punch. Don't know what I'll do with it, but I'll own your cab after I sue your pants off. Oh ... sorry ... I'll bet you don't own your own cab."

Don't engage. This guy is trying to wind you up. Your anger has got you in enough trouble for one day. Get in the car, drive home, take a shower, and go get your kids. It's Christmas Eve. Don't be late.

He hadn't felt in control for two years. He lost a high paying job. Not long afterward Jan filed for divorce. He lost his nice house in the suburbs. But Jan didn't. She lived there with her new husband and Joe's two kids. He knew he should be grateful that the Leslie and Jonathan's routine hadn't been turned totally upside down, but he couldn't fight off feelings of bitterness that inevitably turned to a self-destructive rage.

He landed a pretty good job with a competitor after a couple months of unemployment, but he got canned shortly after. He had always been a great salesman, but a big part of that was his upbeat personality. Now he was a downer. Angry. Suspicious. Surly. The only time he seemed to have control of his emotions was when he was with the kids.

Drive home. Get a shower. Get the kids. Ignore the guy flipping you off and laughing at you. It's not worth it.

Traffic was light but it was going to be tight dropping the cab off at the yard, hopping in his ten-year-old pickup, going home for a shower, and driving over to his old house in time.

Why did I get greedy?

He had taken one more fare, thinking it would give

49

him enough cash to add a few more activities with the kids. And all he got was less than a dollar in coins.

And now he might be a few minutes late. But he didn't want to pick up the kids in the cab. He didn't want any of his old neighbors looking out the window and seeing what he was doing for a living.

Nothing wrong with driving a cab. You could pull in some decent wages—if you weren't paying half of everything in child support.

He drove on, willing himself to relax. He looked on the seat next to him and smiled. A small tom turkey in white plastic with yellow nylon netting to hold the legs in tight. Kroger had a few turkeys left.

One thing had worked out.

God, I'm such a mess. Make this Christmas count. Please.

He shook his head. What did "make this Christmas count" even mean? And when was the last time he prayed?

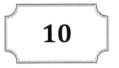

10

Five Hours Earlier

What do you mean your dad isn't home?"

Silence.

"I asked you a question, Donny."

"I'm grounded and now I'm supposed to babysit dad?"

"Don't be smart."

"I thought you wanted me to be smart."

Exasperated, Regina pulled the door shut in the empty patient room, and using all the willpower she had not to shriek, kept her voice to a yell: "Do you know where your dad is?"

"Not exactly."

She sighed.

"What does that mean?"

"I wasn't supposed to tell you anything. He'll be back in an hour or so."

"Your dad told you not to tell me anything? To not tell me where he is? Are you serious? Tell me you are joking."

"Actually, he didn't exactly say it that way. He told me

to turn my phone off so I didn't have to talk to you when you called. And I kind of forgot and turned my phone back on. But I got the distinct impression he didn't want you to know he was out."

"Did we not tell the police you would remain grounded and supervised?"

"I didn't. But I think you and Dad did. But you can take that up with him when he gets back. He said he just needed an hour."

"How long ago was that?"

"Mom, I know I'm gigging you, but everything is fine. I promise."

"I've heard that before."

"Since I'm caught in the middle here, I think I'm going to obey dad's instructions and turn my phone off."

"Don't you hang up on me."

"Turning the phone off isn't the same as hanging up."

Sure enough the line went dead.

Was her son enjoying this as much as he sounded like he was? And where was Douglas? He used to be the most reliable man in the world. Now she didn't know what was going on in his thick skull. Maybe he was having a breakdown. Maybe he was having an affair. He was hard to track down at times.

He's not having an affair. He knows I'd kill him and have the means to do so. And if I didn't, he knows Jason would come back from Afghanistan and hunt him down and do it for me.

Just get back to work, Regina. Things are out of your hands now. Except for here.

It was still slow and quiet in the ER. The only patients she had personally been responsible for were Eduardo with his second-degree burns, and, go figure, Mr. Burns who had suffered a heart attack. That was it.

This was the quietest shift she could remember in years. But that didn't make it an easy shift with everything going on at home. She should have called in for a personal day. She would have been grilled over it, but she had paid her dues. Michelle, her nurse supervisor, would have relented grudgingly, and would have known when to stop asking questions. Regina wouldn't have had to explain that her son had committed two crimes this morning—at least two that they knew of—and was on a short leash with the police to begin with.

She should be home.

Because Douglas wasn't. And he should be. He knew the stakes.

She heard a phone buzzing around the corner. She was being summoned.

You'll turn that phone back on in fifteen minutes and I'll talk to you later Donny. Don't you dare leave that house.

11

Four Hours Earlier

You sure you don't just want to call a cab?"

"No. It's just as easy to drop the car off at the Park-and-Go. It'll be inside while we're gone and I already set it up for them to detail it."

"It's going to cost more to do all that than to get a cab."

"True. But I've already broken the bank on this trip. What's another couple hundred dollars?"

She looked at him in horror, exactly what he was hoping for, and he laughed.

"Stop worrying, Margaret! Enjoy. Other than our kids, we haven't splurged that many times through the years."

"You did buy the car."

"Yes. But I could have bought something like it twenty-five years ago and I didn't. And I've confessed to you countless times that I think I went overboard. I've never had it over seventy-five miles-per-hour, even on the highway. So yes, buying a German performance car was overkill. But it's done. Taking my wife to London to see the Christmas lights, however, is an entirely different matter."

"And how is that different?"

"You … you are priceless."

"Very good answer even if it does come from a television commercial."

"Thank you."

"And you can stop pacing now."

"You know I like to get to the airport early."

"I do too. But we're on the last flight of the day—or the first one tomorrow, depending on how you look at it. I told Betty and Steve we would stop in for their annual Christmas Eve party for a few minutes."

"That's way too far out of the way."

"They're halfway between here and the the airport, Roger. We can stay for an hour and have no problem making our flight in plenty of time. Traffic will be light. You said so yourself."

He paused and stiffened his resolve. Then relented: "Only an hour—and not your usual definition of an hour!"

She reached up and gave him a kiss on the cheek and then frowned.

"What are you worrying about now, Margaret?"

"That white shirt. I know you will snack at Steve and Betty's and I don't want you flying all night in a shirt with a stain on it. Actually I could live with it. But I know it will bug you the whole way over and you won't be able to sleep on the flight, which was the point of taking the redeye."

Roger smiled and walked over to his briefcase. Even retired, he couldn't travel without it. He snapped the clasp open and held up a folded white dress shirt.

"I'm ready for anything that comes my way tonight. Even if it comes with raspberry sauce and whipped cream."

"You always are prepared Roger."

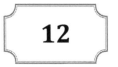

12

Three Hours Earlier

She took a warm bath, not hot, for the baby's sake and safety. She ate something even though she wasn't really hungry. She walked around her apartment a couple of laps. She was cuddled on the couch hugging a heating pad to her abdomen and watching "Elf." Her doctor told her to expect Braxton Hicks contractions. It didn't mean the baby was coming. They were normal in the weeks before the delivery date. She still had two or three weeks to go.

Where are you Brad? I want to read an email from you. I want you to make me smile. I want you to tell me I'm beautiful because after seeing Erica and Danielle I don't feel very beautiful right now. Tell me you're safe.

She felt another contraction. Lower. She felt pressure on her pelvis. It was sharper, stronger this time.

Call my doctor? She said to call if I had any concerns or questions. Any. But should I be concerned? She told me this was to be expected.

Elf's girlfriend and half-brother started singing, "You better watch out" in front of Central Park. His father's wife joined in. She didn't have a very good voice. Holly thought a traditional carol would have been better, but still liked the movie. She would watch "White Christmas" next. It was cheesy but she watched it every year. She and her mom used to sing the "Sisters" song together. She felt sad that she wouldn't be with her mom for Christmas.

First time ever.

On cue her phone chirped. She saw "Mom" on the inbound call data.

"Hi Mom."

"So how is the mother-to-be?"

"Just watching a movie."

"With friends?"

"Not really."

"So no?"

"Nope. I'm alone. But I'm doing good."

"I know how being alone feels. That's all I was trying to tell you before you—"

"Don't start Mom. You've said all this a hundred times. And by the way, you're not with me at a time like this either."

"I can't believe you said that Holly. I've been there for you your entire life. And you know I'll be up there when it's time for the baby to arrive. I wouldn't miss that for the world. But I can't afford to drive back and forth six hours with what I make."

This is where she tells me how hard it was to be a single mom and making ends meet without a college education.

"Mom. I know. And I appreciate all you've done for me. I told you, I'm doing fine. I needed a night alone."

"I'd be there if I could."

"I know."

There was awkward silence.

Why can't she accept I married Brad?

"What are you doing tonight Mom?"

"I just got home. I'm going to heat up some leftovers and watch 'White Christmas' and go to the Christmas Eve service at church."

"Well our evening won't be too different. I'm going to watch 'White Christmas' too. And I'm sure we'll both sing along with Bing and Danny when they sing 'Sisters.'"

"I might have to call you back for that."

"Do! I ... I miss you Mom."

"I miss you too Holly. I don't know why I can't let things go. And I'm not going to nag you. I do like Brad. I just wanted you to be in a better place when you got married and started a family than I was."

"I know. And I understand. I do. But I also know I did the right thing. Even if he did get deployed to Afghanistan and even if I did get pregnant way ahead of schedule."

"You'll be a great mommy, Holly. Better than your mom."

"Mom ..."

"I'm going to start crying, so I'm getting off now. I'll call you back when they start singing and I can be better company."

She didn't apologize and I didn't apologize. But I think we got a little closer to saying a few things that need to be said if the ice formed around our relationship is going to melt. Maybe tomorrow. It's almost Christmas after all. Christmas is the season of new beginnings. New life.

13

Two Hours Earlier

The rage was abating, but not yet gone as tears of grief flowed freely. He pulled into a corner parking lot, blinded by streetlights and the broken floodgate from the corners of his eyes.

It was only an hour ago that it had happened. When it did, he cussed and yelled. He rattled the door. He stomped around the entire house, looking in windows. He didn't care who saw him or heard him. He shouted at God in Heaven in anger; and then in supplication.

He heard nothing in response.

Probably because I couldn't stop yelling.

He had finally got back in his pickup and hit redial over and over on all three numbers: Jan; Leslie; Jonathan. He drove away screaming, "I want my kids!" at the top of his lungs the entire way.

My attorney will be in touch with her attorney. She can't do this to me. She has no right. I'll make her pay.

He finally shouted himself out by the time he was home.

The envelope taped on the front door of the house

he used to call home had his name printed neatly on it, with a note inside.

Fair or not fair, right or wrong, the kids are going with us to see my parents in Ohio. I know you are trying to pull your life back together and whether you believe it or not, we are all pulling for you. Our children love you and don't want to see you hurt. But I don't want to see them hurt any more than they already have been due to circumstances they didn't create. I believe they need to be with extended family, including cousins, in an environment you can't provide right now. I'm sorry for not talking to you ahead of time but I didn't think it would go well and I didn't think the kids' best interest would be served by us fighting. We will be back on the 29th and I will bring the kids over. Merry Christmas—and I mean that.

What can I do?

Possession is nine tenths of the law. In this case 100%.

Nothing. I can do nothing. Just like every other area of my life. I'm helpless and hopeless.

As much as he wanted to keep on storming he knew she was right. Jan's parents had a wonderful home on acreage outside of Columbus. His kids loved being there. They loved being with their cousins.

He looked at the little turkey he bought. There wasn't much else to go along with it. They would be feasting nonstop for the week.

Don't just sit here. Do something.

Joe knew Dennis had pulled the night shift. He had three kids and a wife at home. Joe hoped Dennis knew how lucky he was to have them. And he was about to get luckier.

If he stayed at home, he would undoubtedly feel an old, familiar, caressing tug to head down to the liquor store or a bar if he could find one open. That's what got him to where he was in the first place. He still carried his AA chip in his pocket. When he remembered to touch it he found himself calmer. Problem was he didn't remember to touch it often enough. So he careened through life in a rage. He didn't believe in magic, but he knew that chip meant the first step in getting his life back. The problem was he was so far away from where he'd been. And one step at a time was taking him forever. And there were some things he would never have again. Jan and the kids. That ship had sailed.

Sober for five months. I wouldn't have thought of a drink if I had the kids, he thought bitterly. Now it's all I'm thinking about.

Call Dennis and take his shift. Tell him, "Merry Christmas, you owe me one."

"Joe, St. Joe, St. Joseph, you have made me a hero with my wife—and that makes you my hero. I owe you buddy. I really do. I'll do something for you in return. I promise."

"I got one more thing for you Dennis," Joe had said.

"Yeah?"

"Do your kids like turkey?"

Dennis couldn't believe his luck. He thanked Joe over and over when they met to transfer custody of the turkey from Joe to Dennis.

That made Joe happy. Maybe the happiest he had felt in a long time. But now he was blubbering in a 7-11 lot.

Thankfully a call came in from dispatch. He got his assignment and shifted into park.

My wife ... my ex-wife is right. It's about the kids. She done me wrong. So wrong. But she's so right. And I guess I had the chance to do one good thing today after doing so many bad things.

I didn't know she was pregnant. I swear I didn't know the girl at the coffee shop was pregnant. It shouldn't have mattered. But I worked it out for Dennis to be with his family. And I gave him and his family my turkey. Is that a new start?

14

One Hour Earlier

She stabbed the red off button. Again.

No answer from Douglas. Straight to voicemail with Donny—he had left his phone turned off. No confirmation Douglas returned home and no confirmation Donny stayed home.

Does Douglas not know what is at stake with our son?

The light over Eduardo's room lit up. She padded down the hall and opened the door briskly.

The six-year-old was whimpering. His mom was wiping his brow with a cool washcloth. Regina walked over and looked at the monitors. His vital signs were great. He would be moving to the children's wing of the hospital as soon as a room was prepared for him.

"What can I get you, Maria?"

"The pain seems very bad again," Eduardo's mom told him.

The problem with children patients was knowing how to manage the flow of the pain meds. With adults you gave them a PCA, the trigger for an electronically controlled intravenous infusion pump. The program wouldn't let them overdose, but patients could determine when they needed another shot of analgesic to deaden the pain.

Adults may claim kids are demanding, but that wasn't the case with pain management. They were confused or forgot what to do.

Regina looked at the precious little boy, trying to stifle his tears, but not totally succeeding.

She added a small dose to his drip and caressed his forehead and then his hand. She wanted to give him a hug, but that would not be a good thing to do with second-degree burns. Nothing was tougher to treat than third-degree burns, but nothing hurt more than second-degree burns.

She and Douglas were going to stop with two, then she was pregnant with Donny and that was a good thing.

Eduardo looked at her with grateful eyes. It had been a long time since she had seen that expression in her own baby boy's eyes.

He was last. Youngest. Littlest. Maybe we spoiled him. Maybe we should have stopped calling him Donny a long time ago. But everyone called him Donny. Except for the three friends he had picked up in middle school. They called him Dog or Big Dog.

She cringed every time she heard it.

She asked Eduardo's mom a few questions, told her they would be moving to the children's ward any time, and reminded her to hit the call button if she needed anything. Anything.

She got back to her desk and saw she missed a call. Douglas. He had left a message.

"Won't be able to talk for an hour or two. Trying to connect with Donny. Will talk soon. Love you baby."

Won't be able to talk for an hour or two? Trying to connect with Donny? Where is Donny? What is going on? Something's gotta change.

She hit the speed dial for Donny. Still no answer. She punched red and repeated with Douglas. Straight to voice mail.

I'm going to scream.

She looked down the hall and saw a doctor and two new nurses coming toward her station.

"What's up?" she asked.

"You been busy tonight?"

"It's been light. Real light."

"Well that's about to change."

"What's up?"

"Have you heard the sirens?"

"Not really."

Regina had lived and worked around sirens for more than twenty-five years so she never heard them anymore.

"We've got a fire about fifteen miles from here; the warehouse district downtown. It is going to be one of the biggest fires this city has ever seen."

"Arson?"

"Probably."

"Any estimates on how many people will be coming our way?"

"Thankfully the fire is still nonresidential and all the business are shut up for the night, but we are being told some people are going to lose their homes before Christmas morning is here. Doesn't effect us, but it's going to be bad. St. Elizabeth's is one of three hospitals that the injured will be sent to. We expect most to be from the fire department."

Oh, dear Lord.

She looked at her phone. Using it was about to become non optional.

I hope you know what you're doing Douglas. And Donny, don't you dare leave that house.

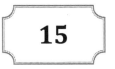

15

One Hour Earlier

Roger, relax, we have plenty of time to make our flight."

"We're supposed to check in for international flights two hours early."

"They aren't going to bar the gates if we're a few minutes late. We'll be there 90 minutes early."

"How fast do you think I can drive in these conditions?"

"The weather report didn't say anything about snow this evening. Just relax honey."

"We'll be lucky to get there an hour ahead of the flight. And I wish this was just snow. Even a heavy snow. It's more like a misty ice," Roger grumbled

"You always get uptight before a big trip. In fact, you were always a bear the last few days before family vacation. I was hoping you planned this one late enough that you would relax and enjoy yourself today."

"I'm not uptight. And I've enjoyed myself until now. But we agreed we would leave Betty and Steve's two hours ago."

"Don't look at me. We were both having fun. You were your usual charming self—not a grizzly bear. I even forgot how much I missed the kids and grandkids and any other problems. For a few moments anyway."

"We don't have any other problems. And I'll admit, it was fun tonight," Roger said grudgingly. "Okay. I'm relaxing. Kind of. I'll stop barking."

"I thought bears growled, not barked."

"What now!" Roger yelled as the car fishtailed through a curve.

A few quick right and left touches on the wheel and the car straightened out.

He opened his mouth and blew out loudly, no longer holding his breath. Margaret's hand was locked like a vice on his upper arm.

"You can breathe now too," he said.

"Okay, we're not going to be ninety minutes early," Margaret said. "So slow down please. And don't worry. We're not the only ones who are going to be running late. And it is the last flight of the day. So we'll make it fine through check in and security."

"Are you sure you have our passports?"

"Yes Honey," she said, patting her coat pocket.

"I don't know what I'd do without you, Margaret. I'd be a mess."

"You would do fine."

He snorted.

"I'll take my share of the blame.," Roger continued. "We should have left Steve and Betty's two hours ago and it was just as much my fault. I hate getting off schedule. I hate being late."

"You always have. We'll be right on time Roger. Don't worry."

It's going to work out, Roger thought. But I hate that time period when you still don't know that for sure. Things always work out.

He looked over and smiled at Margaret but she was looking out the window.

This not being with the kids really does have her down.

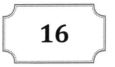

16

One Hour Earlier

She woke with a start.

She yelped as she felt a clinching that would not let go.

Did I wet my pants?

Holly had fallen asleep on the couch. She had turned the TV off and was listening to a Jim Brickman Christmas CD when she drifted off. She wasn't a jazz fan, but Brad gave it to her as a stocking stuffer last year.

She realized she couldn't have wet her pants. There was too much ... too much ... wet.

"My water's broken," she gasped.

She stood up as quickly as the baby would let her. *I have to get to St. Elizabeth's.* Holly had her travel bag ready to go.

I wish Brad was home. I wish he'd sent me an email and told me he still loved me.

She felt like she was wading through mud. Every movement was sluggish—a dull effort laced with sharp pain. Her friend Gwynn from JavaStar said she would drive her to the hospital when it was time. But Gwynn was going to head out of town to see family early evening. She was probably hours away. The baby wasn't due for two weeks.

Why didn't I think about my little guy coming early?

Call a cab?

She felt a moment of relief from the pain and decided she could make the short fifteen-minute drive. She had practiced this numerous times. The car would be freezing. But there was no time to delay. She waddled to the bedroom and pulled up her stretch pants with a grunt of pain. She shrugged over her loosest sweatshirt, not so loose anymore. She aimed her feet and got them into boots with fleece lining. She pulled on her purple cold weather parka that wouldn't zip up all the way anymore, picked up the small travel case, and started down the steps. Halfway to the bottom she had to stop as another contraction seized her.

Is it safe for me to drive?

She half walked, half stumbled to her car. A sheet of ice covered the windshield. She would have to scrape it. She wasn't sure she could. She felt so weak. She began to cry. She needed help. Move forward or backward?

I can't get back up those stairs.

A shiver of panic ran through her.

You can do this.

She sat clumsily in the front seat, her legs still out

the door and on the frozen ground. She fumbled with her phone. She googled taxi companies and hit the first phone number she got to. Acme Cabs. A dispatcher picked up on the third ring. She gave her address and destination.

"I think we have someone close, hold on."

"I'm not doing real well and I have to get to the hospital."

"We'll be there quick as we can."

Please be close.

17

Forty-five Minutes Earlier

He pulled into the parking lot. All the spaces were filled with cars at every angle. It was getting treacherous on the roads. People had slid home as best they could, even if they couldn't accurately aim and land between the white lines.

Yep. Dennis owes me big time.

The makes and models made up a veritable used car lot. They just weren't in perfectly straight rows. The dispatcher said the lady was waiting for him out by her car.

That didn't make sense to either of them. And he didn't see anyone standing around.

It was getting crazy tonight. Too crazy to be on the road. Sirens filled the air in the distance. Huge fire downtown.

He looked around some more. Nope. No one was standing by a car.

Is this a prank call?

The apartments had seen better days. Probably government subsidized. And someone probably thought it would be funny to call for a cab to meet in a parking lot on a freezing cold night—and not be there. That part about needing to be at the hospital was a nice touch.

He drummed his fingers on the dash, humming along on Feliz Navidad.

"I wanna wish you a merry Christmas," he crooned.

I'm trying to get control of my life and wish everyone a merry Christmas, but it's probably not from the bottom of my heart.

Two minutes ticked by.

He drummed his fingers some more, clicked his tongue, and let out a long sigh.

At least he wasn't furious. Not for the moment anyway. He needed to make this a habit. He shifted the car in reverse, rested his arm on the seat behind him, craned his neck as close to a 180-degree angle as he could, and started backing out. The lot was too full and pinched to turn it around and pull out while driving forward.

As he got to the main street in the apartment complex to back out, he stopped for a second, looked down, and hit one of the preset buttons to get away from a jewelry commercial.

"Nothing tells her you love her like a diamond."

He finished the turn and shifted into drive and started off.

What a waste of time. But don't get mad now, Joe. Why should you care? You weren't busy anyway. Bars closed at ten. Flights are all in. Anyone that needs a ride to the airport has already scheduled it. You were just gonna drive in circles and feel sorry for yourself anyway.

He got to the entrance of the apartment complex and braked hard.

Something was niggling at the back of his mind.

You didn't see anything. You were looking for someone. Hard. You were paying attention. Forget it.

He pulled onto a major thoroughfare and headed for an all night diner. No one was around so when he hit the brakes again, he hit them hard, then accelerated to do three full 360 donuts on a usually busy thoroughfare. He actually laughed at that.

When was the last time I laughed?

He drove up the slope and pulled back into the lot, just so he could satisfy whatever was gnawing at the back of his mind. He stepped from the car and left the door open. He'd be back inside in a second anyway. His head was on a swivel as he looked left and right between parked cars. He was almost to the last one when he saw her.

Oh God.

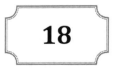

18

Forty Minutes Earlier

Douglas, if you don't call me back, we may be past having Christmas together, much less a merry Christmas. I am so tired of this. I am the only one in this household that works fulltime. And I still do everything around the house. We had the police at our house this morning. The police! And you leave Donny alone. And now you are out trying to find him. This isn't right. This isn't right. I'm blaming you as much as I blame him for this. You are not being a good role model. You need to wake up and do the right thing."

She hit off.

"You okay?"

It was Eduardo's mom.

"Yes, of course, I'm fine."

Wide, coffee colored eyes just looked at her.

"Okay, maybe not so good."

"We are going over to the children's wing now. I wanted to come thank you and tell you how wonderful you are."

"You're the wonderful one, Maria. And your little

boy is such a sweetheart."

"May I give you a hug?"

"Would you please?"

When Maria hugged her, she whispered in her ear, "It's Christmas Eve. Almost Christmas. Just about midnight. Miracles happen. My baby boy is okay. Yours will be okay too."

"How did you know about my boy? Was I that loud?"

"No. But a mother knows."

She hugged her back as hard as she could. "I hope you are right Maria. Thank you. I needed that."

The moment was interrupted by the squawk of the PA. The wounded from the fire department were coming in.

"Dude, you are such a wimp. Ain't no one else on the road. Let's see what this thing can do."

A bottle of cherry flavored vodka made another round from front left to right, from front seat to back seat, from back right to left, and then back up front left where it started.

The heater was on full blast. The sound system with subwoofers in the trunk was up as loud as it could go. The windows were down. The four teenage boys laughed and yelled at the top of their lungs as they hurtled down the city street in a snaky pattern that looked like the path of a downhill skier.

"Turn it up," someone shouted from the back.

"It won't go any louder," the driver screeched back.

"Then drive faster—I'm bored!"

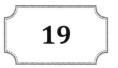

19

Thirty-five Minutes Earlier

Tell St. Elizabeth's emergency room we got a situation," he said to the dispatcher. "Tell them they might want to send an ambulance to meet me. Give them my number. And Frank."

"Yeah Joe?"

"Do it quick. I'm not sure I can get this little lady to the hospital in time. It's not just the baby coming. She fell and I don't know what's hurt or how bad. I was afraid to pick her up."

"Roger that, Joe. You know it's against regs to put an injured person in the cab don't you?"

"Just call Frank."

"I'm on it Joe. And don't worry about me ratting you out. It's a bad rule."

With his luck, he'd probably get canned for doing a good deed. Acme Cab was strict on what he was allowed to do due to legal liability issues. Made it hard to be a Good Samaritan.

No good deed goes unpunished. At least not for me.

How had all this happened anyway? Why did he go

back? He really didn't think he had seen anything. But something urged, then dragged him back to the lot. And how could it be that he would see the same pregnant girl in such dramatically different circumstances in the same day?

The roads were wet and based on the drop in temperature were definitely icy in spots.

Would Dennis have seen her when he pulled in? Would he have gone back if he hadn't?

Was I supposed to be working tonight?

When he found her slumped by her car door he was terrified she was already dead. He shook her by the shoulder gently. She didn't respond. He shook her a little harder and she groaned and rolled into a fetal position as if to protect her baby. That's when he saw the blood on the back of her coat and pants, and streaked on the ground.

He called 911 immediately. The operator that answered let him know there was a five-alarm fire downtown, something he already knew, and it would be at least twenty minutes if not longer before she could dispatch an ambulance; something he didn't know and hadn't anticipated.

"Ma'am, I've got a life and death emergency here."

"I can move her up in the queue but I simply don't have anyone to send at this moment. No one."

City budget cuts. He was all for them until a moment like this.

"If I help, can you stand?"

"I'll try," she mumbled. At least that's what Joe thought she said.

He got his back door open, glad he had kept the car running and the temperature up. He squatted down beside her as low as he could go and got her arm over his shoulder. She wasn't much help but she was such a small thing he was able to lift her from the ground using his legs. He slouched and lurched, half dragging her, as he got her to the backseat. He got her situated with her legs on the ground. He had to go around to the other side, open the door, and pull her back until she was close to lying down.

When she looked up and saw his face he saw a glimmer of recognition. Maybe the whisper of a flinch. She was in pain so maybe the grimace was not personally directed at him. But maybe it was.

I didn't know she was pregnant but I still deserve anything I get.

He slipped and slided out of the parking lot. Need to stick to main roads he thought at the time.

It's Christmas Eve. I'm not with my kids. There's a fire downtown. I yelled at a woman earlier today and now I'm the one taking her to have a baby. Life is strange.

But I did ask God to make this Christmas count. Is that what this is?

He braked at the red light and drummed his fingers waiting for it to turn green. Then he turned left through the intersection and accelerated. He looked right down a side street.

No!

He swung the wheel violently to the left, keeping the front bumper of the charging car from hitting the back door next to where her head rested. No way she would have survived if I hadn't got this thing turned went through his mind as everything continued in slow motion. Blaring music, yelling, and laughter. The car plowed his cab in the back right bumper. The guy came off a side street doing at least fifty miles an hour.

Joe was light headed and knew he was bleeding from his head banging the side window and front windshield in rapid succession. He felt the car spin. Once, twice ... he wasn't' sure how many total times. Not quite as fun as the 360-degree donuts he did earlier.

There was nothing to do but pray they didn't hit or get hit by anything else and wait for the car to stop spinning.

It did. And to his amazement, the car that hit them drove off.

How is that possible?

His car was undriveable. Dead. He was afraid to look in the backseat but he had to. She was breathing. That was good.

He had to figure a way to get her to St. Elizabeth's.

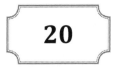

20

Thirty-Five Minutes Earlier

Dude, you gotta stop. Someone might be hurt."

"You push me out the door and get behind the wheel if you want us to stop. I'm not going to jail for this."

"You heard the cop today. We're all going to jail. It's not just you. We're in this together."

"Or maybe they'd send us to juvenile center," a third voice chimed in from the back.

"Just as bad," the driver said.

"This thing aint' going very far. Look at the steam from the radiator. And your bumper is dragging."

"I'm driving this piece of junk as far away from here as it will go. But we aren't stopping except to get some water to put in the radiator."

No one else protested.

Regina longed to call Douglas to find out if he had found Donny. Not possible. It was just before midnight and officially a crazy night in the ER.

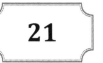

21

Twenty-Five Minutes Earlier

What is that guy doing in the middle of the road?" Margaret asked.

Roger sighed and slowed down. He looked at the clock on the dashboard. They might make their flight still, but not if there was going to be a delay every mile. He thought he could take the midtown express but they were detoured onto busy streets because everything downtown was closed off. Apparently every police cruiser, fire truck, and ambulance in the city had been summoned to an inferno in the warehouse district that had already forced the evacuation of one neighborhood as a precaution if the fire spread.

Where are they going to put all those people? What a way to spend Christmas. We've been so blessed. We just haven't had many problems.

"What do you think is wrong with him Roger?"

"Probably drunk. You'd think people could stay away from the bars one night a year."

"He looks crazy. Be careful."

"No doubt. A lot of people are crazy."

"Steer around him. I don't care if we do miss our plane"

"I am steering around him and I do care if we miss the plane."

"Farther. He looks like he might want to attack us."

"Maggie, if I pull to the side any further I'm going to be on the sidewalk."

"Then drive on the sidewalk," she said sharply.

What was eating her the past few days?

Margaret looked sideways at the man one more time. Their eyes met. He no longer looked crazy. He looked sad. Desperate. Tearful. She couldn't look away until they were twenty yards past him.

She turned her head for one last look backward. He was mouthing something.

Help? Help?

"Roger, stop!"

"I'm not stopping, Margaret. We'll never make it to the airport."

He was back in his own lane and picking up speed.

"Roger, you have to stop and go back. That man needs help."

"You're the one who said he looks dangerous."

Margaret was silent and Roger drove on.

"Roger!"

"Okay, okay," he sighed. "I'm going back. But if things

don't look right, I'm driving on."

"Agreed. But I think we need to stop. I feel it."

He was beginning to accept that they would miss their flight. Guilt gnawed at him. When was he going to tell Margaret he couldn't use his flight miles for first class tickets this close to departure time? He really had paid a small fortune for the tickets. He didn't like to keep things from her.

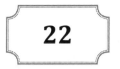

22

Twenty Minutes Earlier

Regina looked at her phone. Six missed calls. Apparently Douglas had finally tried to get back to her when she no longer had a spare second to talk.

All she could do was assume he was with Donny and everything was okay.

Dear God, let it be so.

Saying goodbye to Eduardo and his mommy had been hard. The heart attack victim had been moved to the heart center as well. Then things got crazy. Someone started a fire downtown. At least arson was suspected. No civilian injuries, but already there were first responders being pulled out of the blaze that needed medical attention. Not everyone was being sent to St. E but they were getting their share. Six firemen with a range of burn and smoke inhalation injuries were under her watch.

The phone at her station rang. She picked up and listened for a full minute. She hung up.

"I need you to wheel a bed to the front entrance," she barked at a nurse assistant walking by. Another assistant was in earshot. "I need 124C prepared for a delivery right now—and I need an OB-GYN, any OB-GYN in this hospital down here right now," she yelled to the receptionist. "Right now. Move it people."

When Regina got her drill sergeant voice going, people moved.

The switchboard had transferred the call directly to her station. The woman was clear and concise. What she described was an injured woman minutes from giving birth. She only added one extraneous detail and that chilled her to the bone:

"A group of teens were in a white Pathfinder. The cab driver they ran into is pretty sure they were drunk. Those kids just about killed her. Can you believe it?"

Duane drove a white Pathfinder.

23

Fifteen Minutes Earlier

He unlocked the door quietly and set his duffle down. She was going to be so surprised. Forty-eight hours earlier his CO came to him with glorious news.

"You're going home."

He was instructed to get his butt on a Lockheed C-5 Galaxy—the largest transport plane in the world—that was leaving in three hours and go be with his expectant wife.

"Yes sir!"

"Dismissed."

He gave the shocked but smiling colonel a big hug and said, "Thanks boss. You're the best."

He didn't want to scare her. What if she was sound asleep? Maybe he should have called ahead. But he wanted to surprise her. He didn't have a present but he thought this would be a gift she would appreciate most.

She was all he wanted for Christmas too.

He couldn't believe he would be lying close next to his wife and unborn baby all night.

After a shower of course.

He smelled of travel. The deodorant had given out at least sixteen hours earlier.

He tiptoed to the bedroom door. He would move next to her and whisper her name. She'd know it was him. He wouldn't scare her. They had a connection.

"Holly," he whispered. "Holly-baby. It's me. I'm home."

He turned on the light. The apartment was empty.

Did she go to her Mom's? Was she at church? With friends?

The idea of surprising her was great theoretically, he thought.

But I should have called her.

24

Ten Minutes Earlier

Was he dreaming? His head ached. He thought the bleeding had finally stopped. He looked over. How old could she be? Nineteen? Twenty? Maybe twenty-one?

He felt a stab of pain between his eyes and clinched them tight.

It had been years since he had prayed and he wasn't sure he knew how anymore. He just repeated, "Dear God, we need your help," over and over.

He heard the chirp of a phone again. Not his but he was certain it was in the backseat. Might be someone worried about her.

The nice lady up front had pulled out her wallet and found the girl's driver's license and insurance card. She had given that information to someone in the ER at St. Elizabeth.

He reached into the coat pocket closest to him and pulled out the phone. The call was from Brad. Husband? She wasn't wearing a ring. But sometimes women had to take their rings off in the month before having a baby he seemed to remember. But who knows today. Maybe a boyfriend. Or brother. Or friend. Not her dad. He would be "Dad" in the phone.

He hit the green button but the call had already gone to voicemail.

Call him back?

Someone she knows needs to know what's going on.

He hit the callback link.

"Holly, where are you? Baby are you okay?"

"This is Joe."

"Who?"

"Joe."

"Where's Holly?"

"Who are you?"

"Her husband! Who are you?"

"I'm going to have to take your word for it. This is a good thing, right? You two are together and getting along? No problems? No court orders?"

"What are you talking about? Where is Holly?" he nearly shouted.

"Long story. Do you have wheels?"

"I took a cab from the airport."

"Why are you traveling when your wife is about to have a baby?"

"I've been in Afghanistan! What is going on here?"

"You're at the apartment?"

"Yeah," he said, his voice not so confident anymore.

"We gotta get you over to St. Elizabeth. You're about to be a dad. You are the dad aren't you?"

There was silence.

"Bad question. Sit tight. I'm going to call a friend. We'll get you over here as quick as we can."

"Is she there now? Is everything all right?"

"Long story. Let me make the call. Be watching for headlights in the parking lot."

He put her phone in his pocket and pulled out his own. He punched a preset number. It rang three times before a voice answered groggily, "Hello?"

"Dennis, you know how you told me you owed me big time?"

"Yeah?"

"I need a favor right now. And I mean right now."

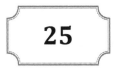

25

Just Before Midnight

Roger slumped back in his car seat, his eyes closed.

"You okay?" Margaret asked him.

"I think I'm ten years older than I was this morning."

"I don't think we're going to make our flight."

"What flight? You know we don't like to travel during the holidays."

She leaned his direction and laid her head against his shoulder. He put his arm around her. They just breathed for a couple moments.

An ambulance drove off. A stretcher rolled by. A young man limped in the ER by himself. They barely noticed.

"You did good Roger. The nurse said she's going to be fine."

"I wasn't so sure."

"Neither was I."

"You get out and go on in, Maggie. I'll park the car. We'll find out. I'm not going anywhere until we know."

He got out of the car to open the door for Margaret.

"You didn't have to do that."

"But I wanted to."

It was a well-practiced routine they had done together for forty years. They both smiled.

As he walked her to the sliding door—he even held electric doors for her—a taxi slid into the emergency lane next to the ER entrance at St. E and smashed the back of his beautiful almost new sleek BMW.

Unaffected, a soldier in desert camouflage and a deep summer tan hopped out the back and ran past Margaret.

Roger and Margaret looked at each other stunned.

The driver got out next. He looked dazed but unhurt. He stared at them in disbelief, shaking his head from side to side. They couldn't help themselves. They looked at each other and burst out laughing.

I don't lie to my wife. I'll tell her I had to buy the fist-class tickets. I just might wait until summer.

I'll tell him tomorrow like I promised myself, Margaret thought. Of course, it's already tomorrow. But I don't want Roger to think about the C-word on Christmas. I'll tell him the day after Christmas for sure.

Postlude

December 25
Just After Midnight

Regina poked her head in room 124C. Less than thirty minutes. Maybe a hospital record. Unbelievable. A beautiful young woman held her baby boy. Next to her was the proudest father she had ever laid eyes on. Just like all of them. Two cab drivers had their butts on the windowsill. They looked uncomfortable but seemed unwilling to leave, even after she hinted that the new parents and baby might want to be alone now.

They don't belong here, but the scene wouldn't be right without them.

A handsome couple somewhere in their 60s was there too. She assumed grandparents but was told they had never met the girl before today.

The strangest Christmas Eve she had experienced in her fifty-two years on earth, Regina thought. She looked at the clock, reminded that the calendar had now turned to Christmas.

St. E's ER did get busy, but not as busy as expected. With the extra staff pulled in everything was under control.

Except her nerves.

What have you done Donny? Were you in the car that hit this girl?

She stepped out in the hall and there were her two men at the end of it, next to her station, sitting in a pair of desk chairs they've pulled together. Their heads were close together. They were in serious conversation and didn't notice her walk up.

Douglas jumped up and grasped her in a bear hug, the one she loved so much. Regina was mad at him and wanted to push away, but couldn't. She rested her face against his chest.

"Sorry about giving you a hard time on the phone," Donny said awkwardly.

"Who is sorry?" Douglas asked.

"I'm sorry, Mom," Donny said.

Now mother and son are both uncertain. Awkward. They manage a sideways hug.

She didn't want to ask but had to: "So where were you before midnight?"

"With dad."

She looked at Donald with surprise. He nodded yes.

"Where?"

"At church. We went to JavaStar and talked a couple hours. Then we went to Christmas Eve service."

"Donald, you about scared me to death. Your

message said you were out looking for him."

"No it didn't."

"You specifically said you were trying to connect with him."

Father and son looked at each other.

"Mom, we were out talking. Trying to connect, you know? Connect."

"You weren't out with your friends?"

"Uh, no. I was grounded."

"And you followed that directive even though your dad was out?"

"He was gone less than an hour Mom."

"About an hour longer than he should have been," she said, now looking at Douglas.

"I had to pick up a present for you and I knew Donny would stay in."

"We agreed we couldn't afford presents this year."

"That's why I brought you this." He handed her a lanyard with a laminated ID that had his smiling face on it. "I don't start until after the New Year, but the new boss said I could pick this up to show you and make it a merrier Christmas."

That's when she lost it and started sobbing.

"Don't get too worked up. It's still a pay cut from what I was making."

"I'm not crying because you got the job," Regina said.

Some of the sobbing was out of guilt for thinking the worst about husband and son. But her sense of relief was overwhelming. Not because her husband found a job, but because she got the feeling that maybe she was going to get her son back. She sobbed because deep inside, hidden away, she was finding some of the joy and peace she hadn't felt in such a long time.

"You came home, Brad."

"I did. To you and my baby boy."

He lifted the bundle from her arms. He had to hold his son again. He marveled at the tiny pink fingers.

"Joe."

"Yeah Dennis?"

"I need a favor."

"I think I owe you one now."

"You do."

"What do you need?"

"A ride home. And you need to back me up on what happened with the boss."

"You got it. I can do that."

"By the way, this is sweet and all. But can we go now?"

"Thank you."

Joe was almost outside the door when he heard the soft words.

He turned toward mother and father and baby.

"I need to say something to you about earlier today," he started to stammer out.

"Please don't," she said. "You saved my life. You saved my baby."

"Doesn't mean that what I did at the coffee shop was okay."

Brad looked from Holly to Joe and back to Holly, puzzled.

"Then just let me say you're forgiven before you ask for it."

"Thank you. I needed that."

"So did I. So do I. I got a few issues of my own to clear up."

"Me and Dennis got to go. But let me just say again, congratulations; you are a beautiful family. Brad ..."

Brad looked up from the baby and into Joe's eyes, brimming with tears.

How many times can I cry in one day?

"Never forget how blessed you are. Never take it for granted."

Brad handed the baby back to Holly to go and shake hands and say thanks to the man who turned around and found his wife in the snow.

But Joe was gone.

Joe knew he was still so far away from where he had been, but he had taken a few more steps on the road back tonight.

"When they saw the star,
they rejoiced exceedingly with great joy."
—

Matthew 2:10, King James Version

Mark "M. K." Gilroy is a publishing veteran who got his start as a sports writer for a local newspaper when he was still a college student. He's done everything in the book industry from packing boxes, ghostwriting, editing, proofing, sales and marketing, and serving as a publisher and senior executive for Thomas Nelson and Worthy Publishing.

His first three novels, *Cuts Like a Knife*, *Every Breath You Take*, and *Cold as Ice*, have received critical acclaim from national publications like *USA Today*, *Publisher's Weekly*, *RT Review of Books*, *Fresh Fiction*, and many others.

Mark's sixth child just headed off for college, so he and his wife Amy are now official "empty nesters" residing in Brentwood, Tennessee.

Connect with Mark at:

mkgilroy.com | markgilroy.com | www.facebook.com/MKGilroy.Author

Made in the USA
Middletown, DE
27 May 2015